Also in the series:

The Secret Lives of UNICORNS

Dr Temisa Seraphini Sophie Robin

For dad, who loved the seaside.
To mum and my sisters, for being as strong and soft as water.
- Anuk Tola

To my mum, my port in a storm.
- Anja Sušanj

The Secret Lives of Mermaids © Flying Eye Books 2020.

First edition published in 2020 by Flying Eye Books,
an imprint of Nobrow Ltd. 27 Westgate Street, London, E8 3RL.

Text © Sangma Francis 2020
Illustrations © Anja Sušanj 2020

Anuk Tola is the pen name of Sangma Francis. Sangma Francis and Anja Sušanj
have asserted their rights under the Copyright, Designs and Patents Act, 1988,
to be identified as the Author and Illustrator of this Work.

1 3 5 7 9 10 8 6 4 2

Published in the US by Nobrow (US) Inc.
Printed in Latvia on FSC® certified paper.

FSC
www.fsc.org

MIX
Paper from
responsible sources
FSC® C002795

ISBN: 978-1-911171-87-4
www.flyingeyebooks.com

The Secret Lives of
MERMAIDS

Professor Anuk Tola   Anja Sušanj

FLYING EYE BOOKS

London I New York

CONTENTS

Dear Reader,

My name is Professor Anuk Tola and I am a merologist at the world-famous School of Merology (SoM).

My first encounter with a merperson, or a mermaid as most people know them, happened at our Atlantic Field Station. I was monitoring and recording important evidence that might be useful in communicating with merpeople, when an actual young merboy paid me a visit to ask me to stop monitoring him! I respected his request and over time I have learned that the best way to communicate with merpeople is to let them take the lead. I have since been across many seas and never stopped in my quest to discover more.

Now, I would like to begin by telling you three things:

1. Most people only know of 'mermaids'. The term 'mermaid' is quite inaccurate to describe merpeople! Just like humans, there is more than just one gender among the merpeople. Their societies are large and varied, and each individual is different from the other.

2. Merpeople are not a simple species. They are highly complex, curious, social, fierce, intelligent and incredibly secretive. It has taken hundreds of years and many merologists to collect the details contained within these pages.

3. Their ocean is changing and so are they, so modern merologists are always finding new ways of working with modern merpeople.

I have traced the merpeople's history and worked with new technology to uncover more about their lives and habitats. Within these pages, you will come to learn about their cities, language, art, science and innovations. Armed with this knowledge, I hope that budding merologists will follow me in my quest to investigate the secret lives of merpeople.

Yours,

Professor Anuk Tola

Part 1
WHAT IS A MERPERSON?

Merpeople are often known in myths and legends as 'mermaids'. They are thought of as wise agents of the sea: intelligent, powerful and keepers of knowledge. A sighting can be incredibly lucky or incredibly dangerous. This is, of course, only a part of the picture. Merologists today know that there aren't just mermaids, but a whole world of merpeople.

The SoM has uncovered tremendous detail about how merpeople have evolved and survive today. In the cold depths of salty waters, we'll plunge into our first encounter with these incredible creatures...

Taxonomy Chart:
Kingdom: Animalia | Phylum: Chordata | Class: Malloid
Superclass: Triopoda | Order: Primanatare | Family: Natarinaedia

The First Merpeople

Around 50 million years ago, merpeople looked very different from the way they do today. The earliest merperson can be traced back to a four-legged, marshland creature. Like all animals, they evolved to survive. As new foods became available, they changed their eating patterns. As new predators emerged, merpeople moved on and adapted to new habitats. Today, they are perfectly suited to their underwater world.

Paluspithecus

Aquatliumeci

Aquilusferus

Paluspithecus
Eocene: 54.8 - 33.7 mya[*]
Small land-dwellers that lived in the swampy areas near sea coasts. These mer-ancestors were small animals that ate plants.

[*]Million years ago

Aquatliumeci
Oligocene: 33.7 - 23.7 mya
By now the animals had become partly aquatic, living half-immersed in fresh water and half on land. They begin to eat fish as well as plants.

Aquilusferus
Miocene: 23.7 - 5.3 mya
Found in fresh and salt water. The spine extends, the ribcage broadens and there is a thicker wall of muscle and skin around the torso. The tail is large and powerful while the legs shorten into side fins.

Modern merpeople

Primanatare

Primanatare
Pliocene: 5.3 - 1.8 mya
Physically much closer to today's species. They are much larger in size and have begun to develop higher intelligence. The side fins shorten with less use. They continue to breathe above and below water. They are one of the top underwater predators.

Modern merpeople
Pleistocene: 1.8 mya – present day
Highly intelligent, sociable creatures that populate seas and rivers across the world. A wide range of adaptions for different tail patterns have developed. They spend almost no time on land but have organs that allow them to breathe above and below the water.

Underwater Marvels

The body of a merperson is a marvellous underwater machine. Built with layers of fat and hair for warmth, they are able to thermo-regulate, which means control their body heat.

Eyes

Merpeople's eyes are adapted to see in both air and water. Their eyeballs are covered in a transparent layer that flicks forward when underwater to protect the eye. Above water, the layer flicks back.

Breathing

Tucked away behind the ears are the gills. These allow merpeople to breathe underwater. Similar to some lungfish, merpeople have an organ that contains a pocket of air. This air pocket stores oxygen, which they can use to breathe when out of the water.

Skin

Incredibly thick, the skin covers a layer of blubber that keeps them extra warm in the cold depths of their underwater world. The skin may appear shinier than human skin. It tends to dry out above water, which is why merpeople prefer not to venture too far on land.

Hair

They tend to grow thick locks and their skin is covered in tiny hairs, barely visible to the naked eye. These are sensitive to any movements in the water. They can sense changes in the water currents and movement from nearby animals. In this way, they can 'see' what is around them.

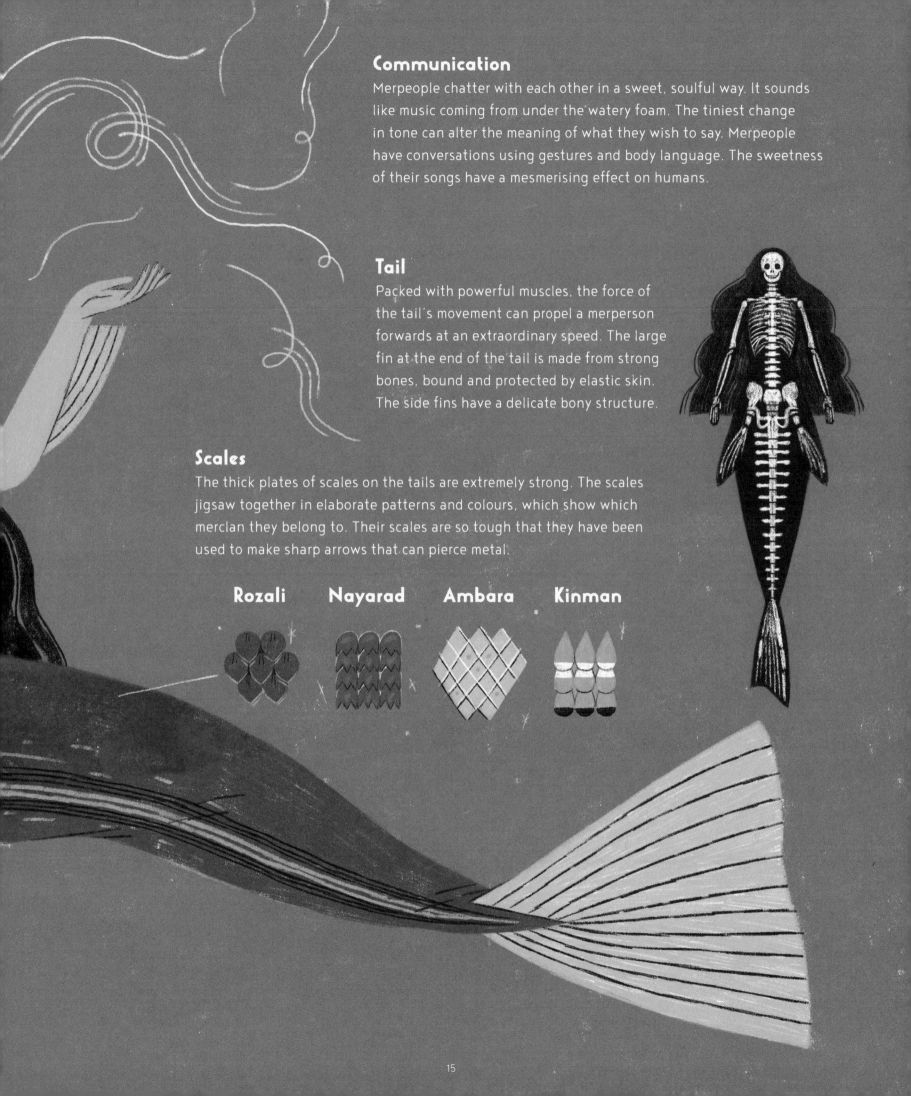

Communication

Merpeople chatter with each other in a sweet, soulful way. It sounds like music coming from under the watery foam. The tiniest change in tone can alter the meaning of what they wish to say. Merpeople have conversations using gestures and body language. The sweetness of their songs have a mesmerising effect on humans.

Tail

Packed with powerful muscles, the force of the tail's movement can propel a merperson forwards at an extraordinary speed. The large fin at the end of the tail is made from strong bones, bound and protected by elastic skin. The side fins have a delicate bony structure.

Scales

The thick plates of scales on the tails are extremely strong. The scales jigsaw together in elaborate patterns and colours, which show which merclan they belong to. Their scales are so tough that they have been used to make sharp arrows that can pierce metal.

Rozali   Nayarad   Ambara   Kinman

Speed and Strength

Merpeople are built to swim nimbly at great speed. They can cut through water much faster than you or I could run across land. The currents help them along and when that's not possible, they must swim against the powerful force. It's not an easy task. Luckily, young merpeople learn different techniques to swim easily in dangerous water.

Body roll

They need great strength in their torso and elasticity in their backbone to roll like a wave as they push forwards. The chest presses into the water, the torso rolls forward and the tail sweeps down and up like a large powerful fan.

Backwards roll

This technique allows the pleasure of observing the light that glimmers on the water's surface. The more playful merpeople skim just below the ocean top so that their tails occasionally flick into the air above.

Side roll

This is a softer and slower swimming pace. It is often used when merpeople swim in pairs so that they can chat casually as they move. It takes time to learn to synchronize with another merperson, so it's most often seen among family and the best of friends.

The torpedo

Curl up, unroll and speed forwards! The torpedo is the power move, and is a lot of fun. Young merpeople love this stroke, sometimes breaking into a torpedo in the middle of a casual swim.

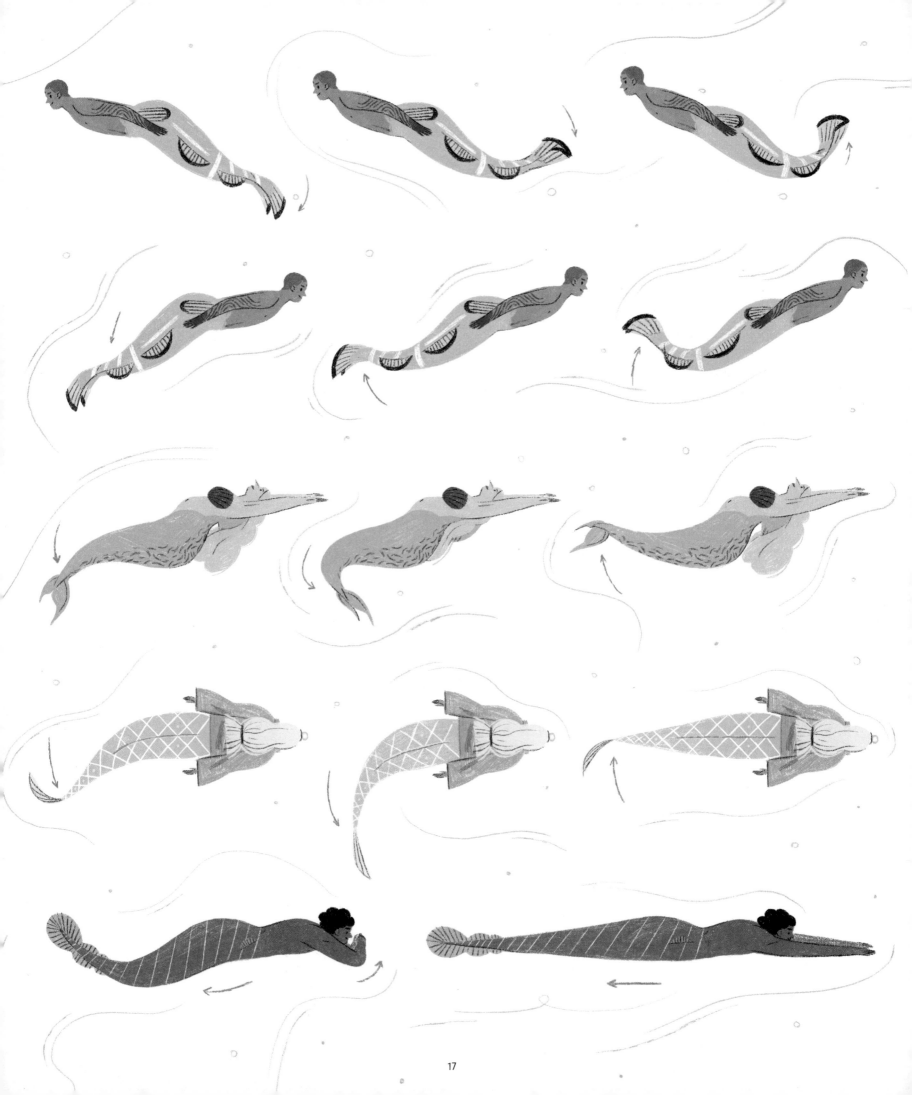

The Life of a Merperson

Merpeople are social creatures that enjoy the company of their fellow merpeople as well as different sea creatures. Family units are very close. They are usually large, and you will often find aunts, uncles, cousins, nieces, nephews and grandparents living together.

Family

The gestation (pregnancy) time for a merwoman is around 10 months. The very young stay with their parents until they are old enough to protect themselves. The life of a merperson is long, active and full of adventure. The very old retire and are then taken care of by their families.

Childhood

Merchildren aren't that different from human children. They begin school around the age of three and learn the basics of life underwater. Merchildren practise swimming every day to become fit and strong against the currents. To navigate the seas where there are no roads or real boundaries, all children learn the Map of Currents.

Growing up

These are the years of exploration and curiosity. Mermaids and merboys enjoy adventuring around the seas and are the most likely to make contact with humans. They experiment with all sorts of haircuts and new styles, which their parents aren't always so pleased with.

Adults and ageing

Merpeople live to be up to 150 years old. They work in the cities of the seas, and the farms of the deeper oceans, until they are old enough to retire and relax. Older merpeople are known to be wickedly mischievous and often play pranks on the young ones.

Part II
MERPEOPLE OF THE WORLD

To travel the depths of all the oceans is an impossible task for explorers. It is so vast and deep, so long and wide, that even the merpeople who live there haven't searched it all. They prefer to gather together in the places they know, in spaces where it is safe and there is plenty of food.

Different groups are known as merclans. There are four that we know of, not including the merpeople of the rivers, but there may still be more out there. These merclans have built noisy cities, written their legends across cave walls and have traded with each other across the oceans. They each have a unique culture and distinctive appearance.

The Rozali of the Atlantic

Where the sea is blackest and the waves rise up to 20 metres high, you will find the Rozali. They are not only known for their strength, but also their knowledge of the strong Atlantic currents. They wear protective sea rock helmets and cover their skin with hardened plates of shell, bone and sand.

Diet: Sea moss, krill, reed jelly, ice fish

Location: Southern Atlantic Ocean

Leader: Eleezah, a generous and kind merwoman

Sea rock helmet

Rozali scales
Dare to use the scales and see the measure of your heart

22

The Soul of a Sailor

Many sailors are terrified of merpeople but none are more feared - or more respected - than the Rozali. It is said that the young merpeople of the Rozali clan lead expeditions to ships in danger. As the wild Atlantic waves rise up, they take hold of the boats and weigh each soul on board. 'Good or bad', asks the ocean and the Rozali listen carefully. The ships of good-hearted souls are steadied and steered to safety. For the bad-hearted, the Rozali offer a deal; a heart for a life. Many sailors have landed on new shores without a heart.

The Nayarad of the Pacific

The Pacific Ocean plunges deeper and stretches wider than any other ocean on Earth. In some parts, its floor falls away into deep, cavernous hollows. In others, volcanoes rise angrily from the sea floor. The Nayarads are adventure-loving merpeople who find their home in this dramatic landscape. They can be recognised by ornamental belts of shell and colourful rock.

Diet: Sea plums, purple weeds, crab claws, smoky moss

Location: Pacific Ocean, near Hawaii

Leader: Niloc, an intelligent and stern but warm merwoman

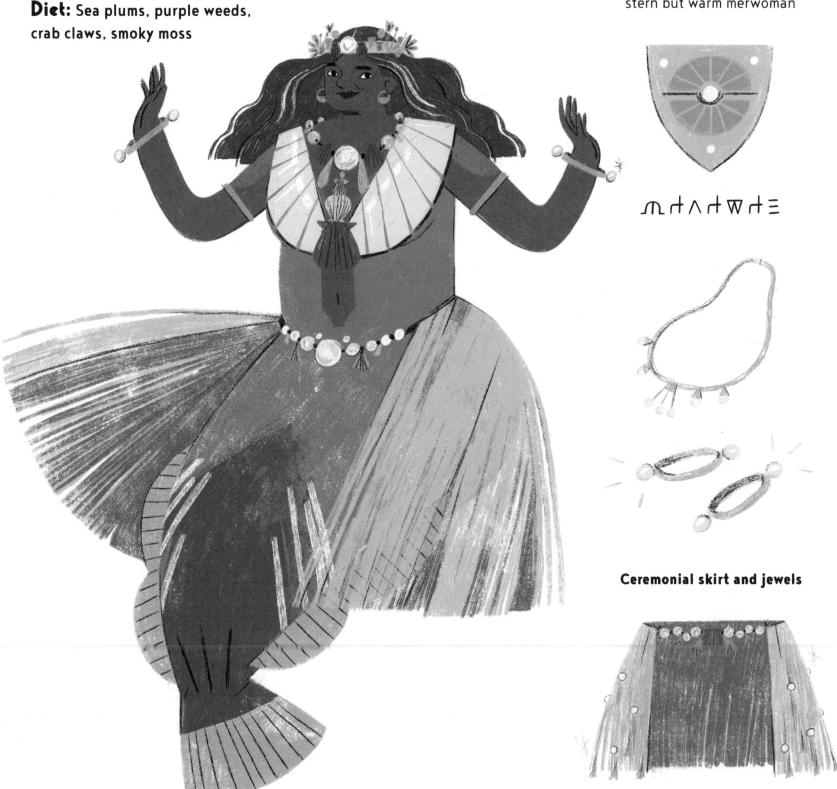

Ceremonial skirt and jewels

Master Jewellers

The land of the Nayarads is a treasure trove of the finest shells, pearls, fish and rocks. They are master jewellers that can make a pebble gleam like an opal. In order to make such dazzling jewellery, the Nayarads take care of their environment. They are highly protective of their coral forests and glittering reed meadows, which attract sting rays, manta rays, snub-nosed sharks, turkey fish and sea cucumbers. To make good jewels, they say, you need the blessings of a thousand fish.

The Ambara of the Arctic Ocean

The Arctic Ocean is a cold, dark and torturous place, where shrieking winter winds can be heard deep in the water. Very few merpeople settle in these parts, but the Ambara are tough. A thick covering of muscle and fat protects them from the freezing waters. They wear protective skins and fur cloaks. Their tails are icy blue and their hair is as white as pearl.

Location: Arctic Ocean, Greenland and Northern Canada

Leader: Ondine, quietly wise, with a mischievous laugh

Diet: Shrimp ice, cuttlefish, krill, yellow seaweed

The Walrus King's Crown

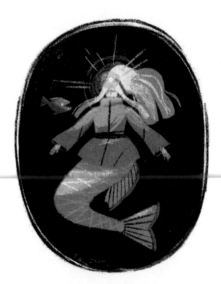

An Ambara pearl lighting up the depths of the sea

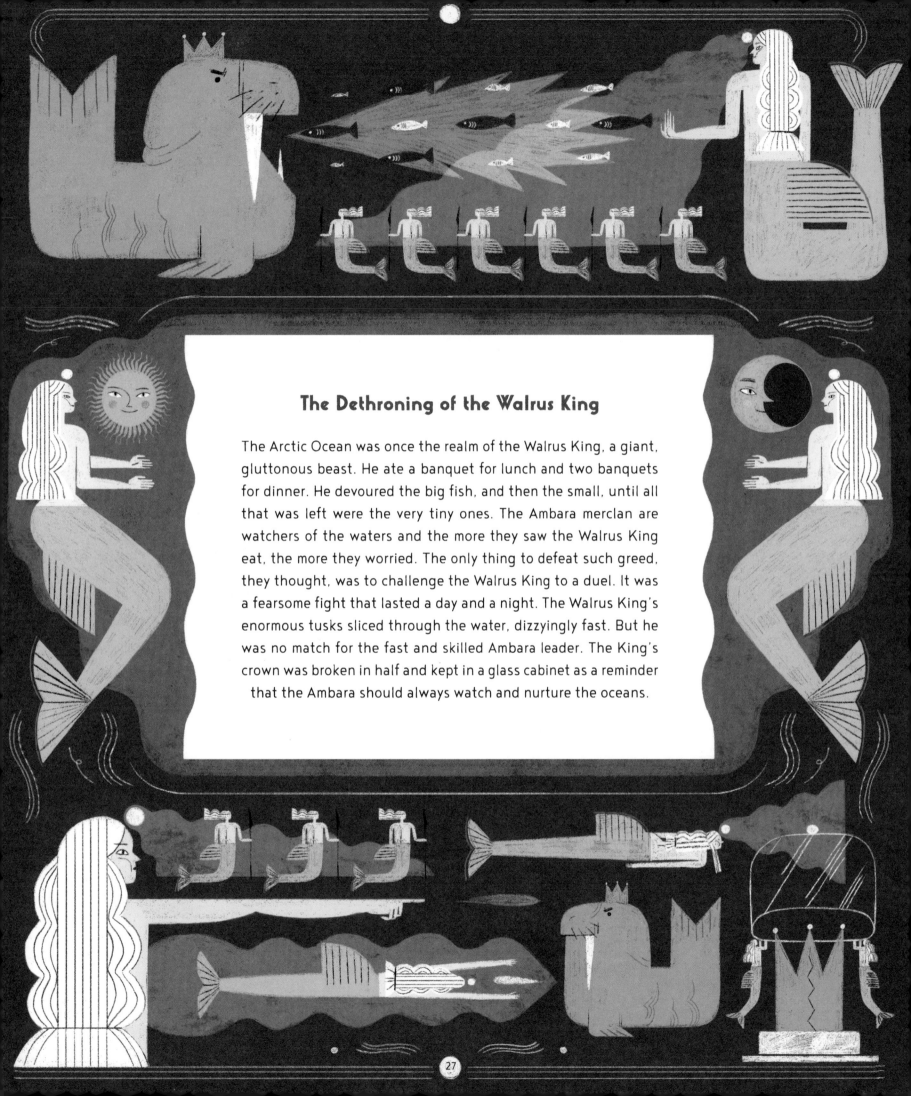

The Dethroning of the Walrus King

The Arctic Ocean was once the realm of the Walrus King, a giant, gluttonous beast. He ate a banquet for lunch and two banquets for dinner. He devoured the big fish, and then the small, until all that was left were the very tiny ones. The Ambara merclan are watchers of the waters and the more they saw the Walrus King eat, the more they worried. The only thing to defeat such greed, they thought, was to challenge the Walrus King to a duel. It was a fearsome fight that lasted a day and a night. The Walrus King's enormous tusks sliced through the water, dizzyingly fast. But he was no match for the fast and skilled Ambara leader. The King's crown was broken in half and kept in a glass cabinet as a reminder that the Ambara should always watch and nurture the oceans.

The Kinman of the Indian Ocean

The Kinman live near the Java Trench of the Indian Ocean. The warmer waters can be as clear as glass, so the Kinman create camouflage to help them remain hidden from divers or fishermen. Their armour is a purple moss and they spread colourful sediment called globigerina across their arms.

Diet: Phytoplankton, curly seaweed, sea grass stems, jellied moss, kelp root

Location: Indian Ocean, Indonesia

Leader: Tiama, a merman of very few words, gentle and watchful

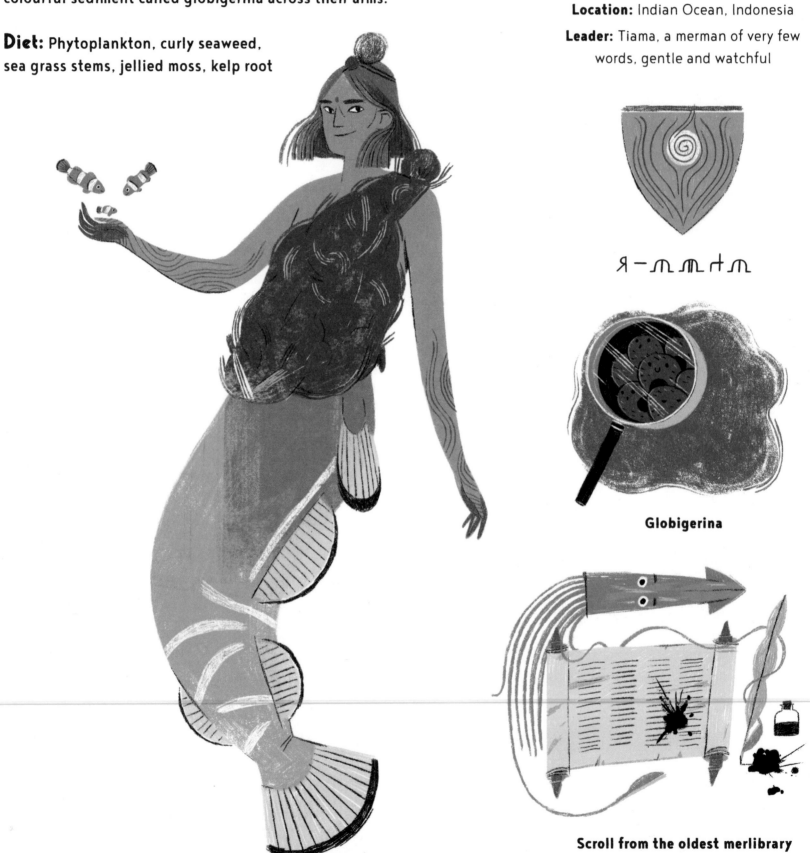

Globigerina

Scroll from the oldest merlibrary

Keeper of the Merlibrary

The Kinman are protectors of the oldest merlibrary. Deep in the Indian Ocean, there is a small hut at the entrance of the library, inside which lives the oldest Kinman. His name is Iai of the Deep. He has one eye and one tooth and a glinting smile. He is the guardian and keeper of merlegends. He totters around the reed gardens, keeping his one-eyed watch for marauders, crooks, thieves and humans! He may seem frail and harmless, but Iai of the Deep is a powerful merman. He can even conjure storms! Every year, on the coldest day of the year, merpeople give him a pearl and thank him for guarding their stories.

Freshwater Merpeople

Smaller clans of merpeople have been sighted dipping through muddy rivers in the company of dolphins, crocodiles and eels. How they got there, and why they chose to be so close to humans, is still a mystery to merologists. Their groups are so small that they have not formed merclans. Our studies show that they have adapted to stay above water for longer than merpeople of the oceans.

Golden mermaid | Ponds and lakes
Recognised by their fiery gold hair, bodies and tails. They have short, sharp spines sticking out of their backs and like to wear pearls. These merpeople adapt to their surroundings, growing large when in lakes and very small in ponds.

Pernix | Waterfalls and rapids
The Pernix like to hide in the Amazon's many winding tributaries. Most sightings have been at night, where they have been seen playing in the bubbling waterfalls. Their tails are a mottled pink and brown.

Galumphs | City rivers

These minuscule mermaids dip through the black waters collecting metals, gold and jewels that have fallen into the rivers. Their eyes have an amber glow and their hair is often red. They wear metal armour that looks like twisting sculptures across their backs.

Baraudites | Wetlands

These merpeople have distinct leathery green tails, similar to a crocodile's. Sightings across the wetter areas of Australia and the Congo show that they prefer slow-moving waters where there is lush plant life.

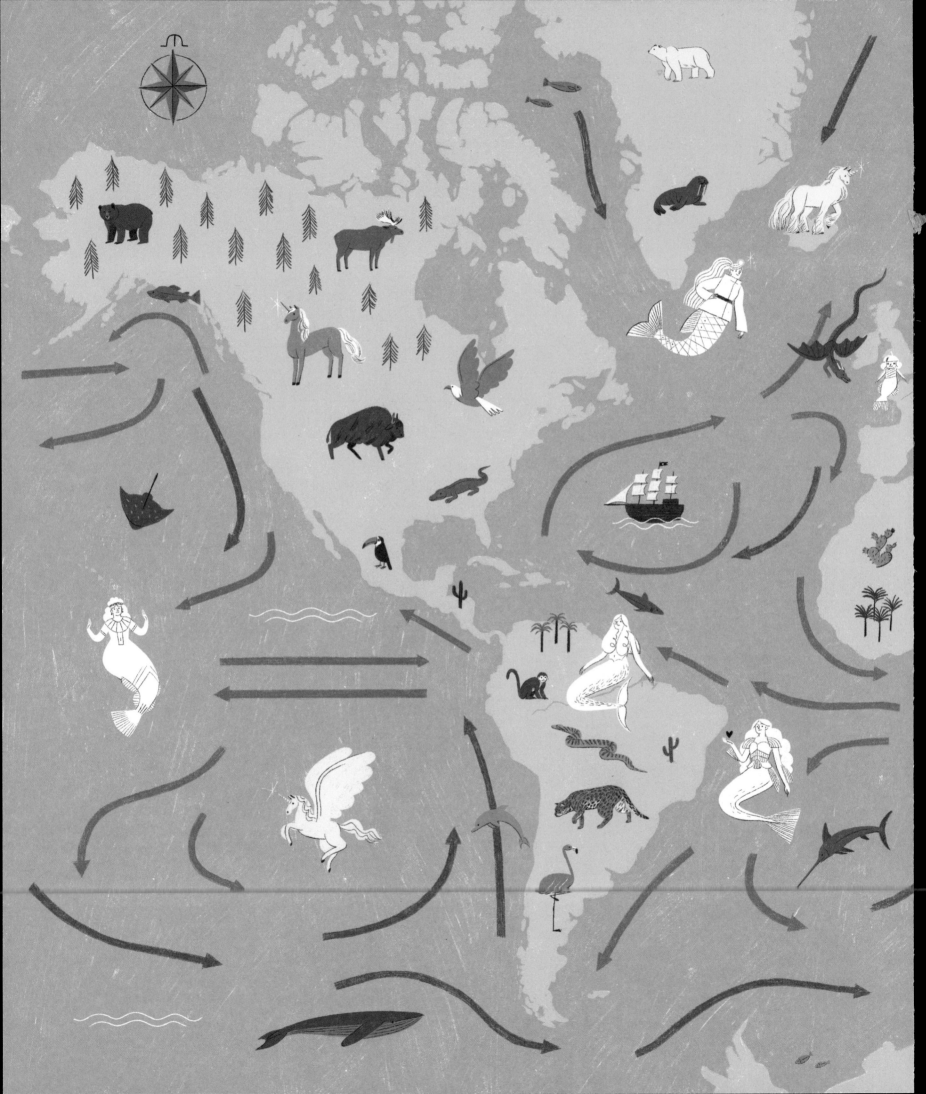

Map of Currents

The winds that circle the world push the water currents in fixed patterns. To travel great distances, it is better to swim and sail to the rhythm of these winds. Both merpeople and sailors know these maps like a print in their minds. The thrust of the water changes throughout the year.

Part III
WHAT WE KNOW ABOUT MERPEOPLE

Many students who come to the School of Merology already know about the meetings between humans and merpeople. Some have even heard the stories of mersongs that have lured sailors to a watery end. But what do these tales actually tell us about merpeople? Are there other ways we can learn about these mysterious creatures?

This chapter will take a look at how merpeople have been recorded through human history. We will reveal the surprising and ingenious ways merpeople live underwater and slowly piece together the history of mercivilisation through using modern technology.

Legends

Merpeople have gone by many names to us land-dwellers. They have been called nixes, sirens, oceanids, muirs, merrymaids and of course, mermaids. They became symbols of good luck and ill-fortune. These are some of the most famous accounts of merpeople given by humans.

Merrymaids

Padstow is a bustling port on the coast of Cornwall, England. Legend has it that a merrymaid (the local word for merperson) liked to visit the waters near the port. One day, a man named Tom shot her accidentally, thinking she was a seal. As her dying curse, she created the Doom Bar, a strip of sand that blocked the harbour and wrecked many ships trying to reach land.

Rusalki

In Russia, there is an old Slavic legend about young water spirits called Rusalki. Although they were once thought to bring good luck for those planting and farming new lands, over time the Rusalki became feared. They became devilish in nature, singing taunting songs and dancing in the waves to lure lost souls.

Ningjyo

In Japan, merpeople are called Ningjyo, which translates as 'human fish'. The Ningjyo are said to cry tears of pearls and will give the power of eternal youth to anyone who eats their flesh. The first recording of Ningjyo in Japan was made by the Empress Suiko in BCE 619. She captured a mermaid and put her in a tank for people to come and see.

Yawk Yawk

In Arnhem Land, Australia, a group of water spirits live in sacred river bends,
in the east, west and south Alligator Rivers. These are the Yawk Yawk, guardians
of the waterholes. They are night-wanderers who rise from the water to explore
the land. The Yawk Yawks are great art lovers. They find ways to inspire
human artists, and sometimes even collaborate with them.

Gods of Water

Many human gods have been associated with the seas. Sometimes they have taken the form of merpeople an appeared to humans to remind them of the power of the sea. It is unclear whether merpeople themselves have ever worshipped these gods.

Polynesian Goddess of the Sea

Tangaroa, Goddess of the Sea, held Earth's water inside her body. When she could no longer hold it in, she let it burst across the dry lands and created the oceans.

Babylonian God of Water

Enki, son of Nammu and God of Water, lived in the ocean underneath a place called Azu. He was known to be a mischievous god who wore a cloak of water, alive with glittering fish.

Nigerian Goddess of the Ogun River

Yemaya, Goddess of the Ogun River, was a kind and giving goddess who wore seven billowing skirts of blue and white. In the language of the Yoruba, her name means Mother of the Fish. She travelled down to Earth from the sky on a length of rope, with 16 other gods.

Roman God of the Sea

Triton, son of Poseidon (the Roman god of the Sea), is famous for the sea conch he blew to control the waters. He was known as the messenger of the seas and lived in a golden palace deep in the ocean. Its whereabouts is still a mystery.

Assyrian Goddess of Water

Atargatis, Goddess of Water, was once worshipped in a temple with a golden roof, which now crumbles off the coast of the Mediterranean Sea. It is said that she kept pet fish in a sacred lake.

Language and Communication

Merologists take a serious interest in the study of merlanguage. Merwriting uses symbols with lines, triangles and circles. The symbols are much like our alphabet, with 26 letters that represent different sounds. Deciphering an unknown language is an almighty task and for many years merologists had no way of knowing what the words said – until 1504 when merologist Patty McBane finally cracked the code.

Cracking the code

McBane was a true language detective and loved to use codes. As merpeople are very fond of writing, she found many examples to puzzle over. The key was the discovery of a piece of rock that told the story of an underwater queen. The story was carved in merlanguage, but astonishingly, also had a faint carving of text that was similar to an old human language called Latin. It was the missing piece that meant she could finally crack the code.

Try and solve the hidden messages throughout the book with this helpful guide:

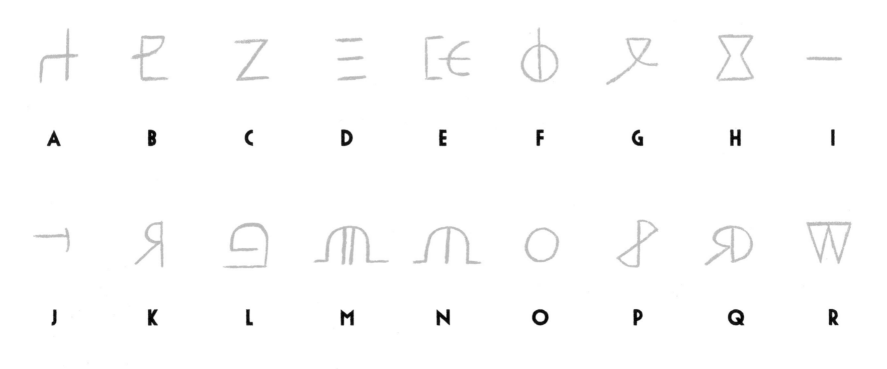

The Ceiling of Earth

The most impressive temple to merlanguage is called the 'Ceiling of Earth'.
It is a beautiful stone dome carved out of the rock at the bottom of the
Black Sea. The cave covered by the famous Ceiling is thought to have been
a workshop where the merpeople's books were created. The parchment-like
material of merbook pages is made from fish skin that has been de-scaled,
stretched and coated in waxy blubber. The text is etched onto the skins
with small nicks, grooves and stamp-like markings.

43

Art and Music

Merpeople are incredibly fond of art. Underwater museums burst with delicate sculptures, ornate jewellery, living reed tapestries and polished rock displays. These much-admired collections draw visitors from far and wide. some pieces of art have become icons of merculture.

Triton's Conch

A magnificent shell of polished pearl and silver. It was owned by the great god Triton, who wore it proudly around his neck. Triton could use it to make waters completely still, or raise them into treacherous waves.

The First Prince's Diadem

This grey, gnarled-looking crown resembles nothing more than a rock, unless worn on the right head when it transforms into a circlet of sparkling ice. It was a gift to the first prince of the Balangytes and once gleamed so bright, it looked like the pearlescent horn of a winged unicorn.

Tapestry of the Waves

Red, purple, blue and white water flowers have been cleverly woven together to craft a tapestry that appears to pulse and curl like a wave about to break.

The song of the Mer

Merpeople are trained to sing from a very early age and most adults belong to
a local choir. Merpeople can often be spotted practising their songs above water,
where they can train their lungs to expand in the air. Their vocal range can
go from a high trilling pitch to a deep bellow that pushes the water sideways.
A highly decorated book of mermusic was discovered washed up on the coast
of France. Its detailed, colourful pages led merologists to believe that it must
have once been owned by a family of great importance.

Science and Innovations

Just as humans have come up with inventions that make life on land easier, merpeople have found ways to make the most of their watery realm. Just like humans, their inventors were incredibly clever.

Currents predictor

Like a weather vane, the currents predictor shows changes in the strength and direction of the ocean's currents. This helps merpeople to predict where the current will take them and how quickly.

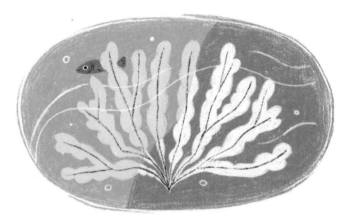

Bladderwrack grass

A particular sea grass called bladderwrack turns from a glorious yellow to white when the water becomes dirty. On discovering this, merpeople planted them around the towns so that they knew when it was time to move into cleaner waters.

Upside chambers

This invention is a large air bubble used to practise above-water breathing. It is essential to practise this many times to get used to the different breathing technique. It would not be wise to try it for the first time in plain sight of humans.

Bubble lens

A drop of water held still in a bubble of air, the bubble lens shows distant objects in immense detail. A highly useful device when keeping an eye out for predators! Smaller versions have been adapted for merpeople to wear to help with poor eyesight.

Farming and Gardening

Merpeople build farms and gardens designed to draw the attention of fish. These are full of tiny plants and krill that attract the fish that merpeople eat. Merpeople also build lovely gardens with rock walls that house goose barnacles to attract jellyfish. Merpeople keep the luminous jellyfish to light up the dark water, and as pets. They feed and wash them, and when the sun sinks, the creatures begin to cast a luminous glow that is bright enough to garden by.

The First Mercivilisation

The first great mercivilisation was the Balangytes. They were led by women, and the long line of Queens ruled with a strict but fair outlook. Under one peaceful banner, they brought together merfamilies to build bigger communities, began underwater farming and constructed dazzling cities with buildings covered in shell and glittering rocks. Their empire built up slowly into a civilisation that spanned the vast ocean floors.

Archaeological finds

Merologists first discovered the cities of the Balangytes when one of their sculptures was found half-buried in the sand of the seafloor. Merpeople and merologists have worked together to unearth many incredible artefacts and buildings from the ancient civilisation. Some of the smaller objects can be seen in the School of Merology's museum.

Living together

Dhakkina, the capital of the Balangytes, was made of impressive teetering towers where many families lived together. These towers were lashed together and had anchors that were driven deep into the ground to keep them from moving too far. It is now abandoned and looks like a ghost city. It is nothing more than a play park for the fish.

Keeping records

The Balangytes kept extraordinarily detailed notes on everything, including neighbourly disputes, new inventions and daily shopping lists. One young Balangyte prince was an avid note-taker. He even recorded what he ate for breakfast every day. By sifting through the crumbling stone tablets left by him and other Balangyte writers, we have come to understand more about the first merpeople.

Cities

Beneath the still, glassy top of the ocean, there is a wondrous buzz of life in the towns of the merpeople. But an underwater city is not an easy thing to build. The tiniest of details need to be considered. There's drift and currents to think about, as well as transportation and, of course, decoration.

First mervillages

The first mervillages are believed to have floated gently along with the currents, going whichever way the water took them. But this, inevitably, had problems. First, it was unimaginably difficult to arrange a visit with relatives when your house never stayed in the same place. Secondly, merpeople had not yet worked out how to predict the tides, and on many dreadful occasions, villages were sent crashing into each other.

Building mastery

The great builders and architects of the seas engineered new ways to overcome this tricky issue. We know from missions underwater that there are now bathhouses, dance halls, schools, museums, glittering palaces, market squares and barns. The largest cities are built into the trunks of great kelp forests. The huge fronds rise up so high from the ocean floor that if you were to stand at the bottom, you would look like an ant beside a tree. In these forests, the houses are lashed into the towering weeds.

Rock houses

Where kelp does not grow, merpeople have cut houses in to the coastal shelves. These look like buzzing beehives with domes hollowed into the rock. The great pillars and arched ceilings look like underwater cathedrals.

Shipwreck shelters

For the remaining bands of travelling merpeople, there is shelter to be found in old shipwrecks and the hollows of sea caves.

Part IV
MEROLOGISTS, MERPEOPLE AND YOU

The merologists at the SoM take extraordinary care to watch the oceans and rivers for movements and messages from the merpeople. It's no easy task when there is so much to inspect, but we try to leave no rock unturned and no water cave unexplored.

At the SoM it is our task to gather the reports, discuss our discoveries and make contact. In the last few years, merologists have made huge progress! We can now work closely with modern merpeople to understand more about their world.

And this is where you come in...

Famous Merologists

The first merologists were sailors and coastal dwellers. These people understood the sea and its wilder nature. At this time, they saw many mermaids but did not know that there was a whole world of merpeople. Nowadays, merologists know far more and have become experts in other fields, such as history, coastal maintenance and underwater technology. Some of the most pioneering professors have portraits in the SoM's Great Library.

Patty and Paul McBane
Cryptographer and book antiquarian (1420–1510)

Patty and Paul worked together to uncover the mysteries of new text, codes and cyphers. Paul was a fond collector of ancient texts, parchments and bound manuscripts. Together they spent hours unlocking the language of the merpeople. They finally solved it in 1508, just after their 88th birthdays.

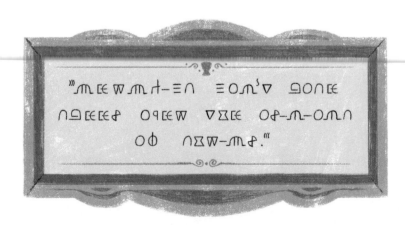

El Beccio
Art historian (1848–1913)

El Beccio founded the fabulous Museum of Mer in London. She spent years saving the art of merpeople from destruction. Over this period, she studied the artworks to understand more about their myths, stories and legends. She was a great storyteller and incredibly funny. She firmly believed in sharing the stories of merpeople with as many humans as possible.

She ended every story by saying; 'Merpeople shy from us because we don't understand them. The more I know, the more I hope to become their friend.'

Captain von Winterfield
Sailor (1665–1757)

A master sailor whose dedication to understanding merculture saw her sail around the world 20 times. She collected valuable data about the different merclans and their whereabouts. She also took water samples wherever she went, trying to understand if there was a pattern between water quality and merpeople's existence. She was the first to discover that merpeople keep clear of polluted waters.

Torin Tomalin
Swimmer (1850–1945)

Torin could swim as fast as a typical merperson. He could hold his breath for over 20 minutes and trained himself to dive 5 metres deep. Before underwater technology was invented, Torin was able to collect and examine much of the underwater relics left by merpeople.

A World in Danger

The clear sparkling waters that merpeople call home are in danger from pollution. Bits of plastic and rubbish are sinking into the sand and clogging up their cities. Merologists have discovered whole families, old and young, escaping into the Realm Beyond – a place of magic, home to creatures that need safety. It is a place that can be entered if you know where to look...

The Realm Beyond

You might find the entrance behind a bushel of innocent-looking seaweed or under a small cluster of rocks. Not many people know how to find it; not many people notice the innocent-looking seaweed, but merpeople do. Merologists only came to discover its existence in 1922 after closely monitoring a group of merpeople in the Indian Ocean. They found a large family of merpeople abandoning their home to start a new life there. Mythical and magical creatures have always known about its existence, but it is being used more as the seas become unclean and unsafe to live. But not all merpeople want to move. Many stay in the cities and work hard to push away the rubbish that collects near their homes. Modern merologists must find ways of keeping them safe in our seas. Our work now is more important than ever.

Ocean Defenders

A group of mermaids from the Nayarad clan were the first to realize that they needed to break old habits and find a way to communicate with humans. The first step was to find humans that they could trust and who would listen and take action. After a few miscommunications, they found some like-minded humans who also cared about the oceans – the Ocean Defenders.

Beachcombing

All merologists are expert beachcombers. It is one of the most effective ways to find mermaid artefacts while also removing litter from the beaches. When beachcombing, look out for broken pottery, glassware, pieces of gold or expertly made jewellery. These could all be important evidence of merperson craft.

Biological Field Centre

Over the years, the Ocean Defenders have worked with merologists to set up the Biological Field Centre. This thriving hub of research for ocean safety reaches down through the water to the sea floor. The glass building is made up of water and air chambers so that humans and merpeople can both use it. Here merpeople and merologists study water quality, rocks, coral, sand and sediment, fish behaviour and plant growth. By working together, they are trying to make the seas clean once again.

How to Become a Merologist

Becoming a merologist is no easy task. But by reading this you are already one step closer. So grab your backpack, hold up your rubbish picker and with these steps go forwards.

1. You must be willing to spend a long time studying the seas and coast. Take note of animals, plants and rocks. Record your findings in a notebook. This could become a future merologist's guide.

2. You need a keen eye for detail. Always inspect things closely and never immediately accept what you see on the surface. The sea contains many depths, and merpeople know how to use these.

3. Learn about merpeople and their history. This will help you understand them. It may even help you learn more about humans!

4. Paddle and swim. You must learn to make the sea your friend. Learn its strengths, nature and personality. Be safe and stay with an adult. Humans do not have the water strength of a merperson. Even a merperson respects the water's power.

5. Never give up. Merology is a challenging area of research and you may sometimes feel out of your depth. With time, you'll embrace the difficulties of navigating merculture. Good luck!

Continuing the Journey

There is an old saying among the merpeople: if the current ahead looks choppy and dark, bring the lamp that lights it. That is to say, some things may be difficult, but that does not mean we should stop doing them. There is still so much to find out about the lives of merpeople and what they get up to in the ocean deep. Take all the knowledge you have read and then read some more. You can make a difference. The School of Merology is waiting for you.

I would like to thank all merologists, both young and old, who have helped me pull this book together. This book is for you, and everyone like you. To Nicole, Professor of Archives, for checking the records in the libraries. To Caroline, Professor of Mer-art for opening my eyes and showing me the most dazzling pieces. To my mother, for preparing my favourite mer-recipes. To my father, for taking me to the sea before I could even swim. My warmest gratitude goes to the students at the School of Merology for taking part in the expeditions for water observation and sanitation. Their sweet-natured determination through wind, rain and fog is a marvellous thing and will help to bring us closer to the wonderful world of merpeople.

Yours,

Professor Anuk Tola